For Arlo

First U.S. edition 2018

Library of Congress Catalog Card Number pending
ISBN 978-0-7636-9949-9

18 19 20 21 22 23 TWP 10 9 8 7 6 5 4 3 2 1

Printed in Johor Bahru, Malaysia

This book was typeset in Times New Roman.
The illustrations were done in ink and watercolor.

TEMPLAR BOOKS

an imprint of
Candlewick Press
99 Dover Street
Somerville, Massachusetts 02144
www.candlewick.com

Sam Usher

SUN

templar books
an imprint of Candlewick Press

When I woke up
this morning,
it was sunny.

I couldn't wait to go
on an adventure.

I said, "It's hotter than broccoli soup,

hotter than the Atacama Desert,

and hotter than the surface of the sun."

Granddad said, "It's the perfect day for a picnic."

So we gathered the necessary provisions.

Granddad would navigate. I would be the lookout.

He said, "Let's find the perfect spot."

The sun beat down.

Granddad said,
"Let's have a rest."
And I said,
"What are we
looking for, Granddad?"
And he said,
"Somewhere picturesque."

So Granddad navigated and I looked out.

I said, "What about this way, Granddad?"

The sun beat down.

Granddad said,
"Let's have a rest."
And I said,
"What else are we
looking for, Granddad?"
And he said,
"Somewhere in the shade."

So Granddad navigated and I looked out.

I said, "What about
this way, Granddad?"

We walked for miles.

Granddad said, "Let's have a rest."
And I said, "What else are we
looking for, Granddad?"
And he said,
"Somewhere
with a cool
breeze."

So Granddad navigated and I looked out.

I said, "What about this way, Granddad?"

The sun beat down.

I said, "Look, Granddad,
what about over there?"

But someone else had found
the same spot.

So we helped
them gather
their provisions.

And then
we shared
the perfect
picnic!

Back at home, once
we'd cooled down,
Granddad said,
"If you keep looking,
you never know
what you might find."

And I agreed.

I hope it's sunny
again tomorrow.